ASHES
ON A
DISTANT
WIND

YOLANDE KLEINN

Published by
Yolande Kleinn, 2021

www.yolandekleinn.com

Ashes on a Distant Wind
By Yolande Kleinn

Cover Design: Yolande Kleinn
Cover Photo: Arto Marttinen
Cover Font: Bruss from thehungryjpeg.com
Interior Font: Born from thehungryjpeg.com

First Edition September 2021
Printed in the United States of America

Print ISBN 978-1-946316-21-9
Digital ISBN 978-1-946316-11-0

For Jazz – Thank you for sharing your incredible heart and energy. Blessed to have you for a friend.

ASHES ON
A DISTANT WIND

The radio in his hand crackled, and Donovan Riggs pressed the button to transmit. "Where the hell are you?" he demanded, sharp with impatience. The radio gave another sputter of protest as it grudgingly cut through static.

"Don't get snippy," came the cheerful retort. Beau sounded even younger over the radio than his twenty-two years. "I had to go the long way round. Fresh debris. I'm almost back to your location."

Riggs swallowed a curse as he set the radio down, dropping it beside the torch that had run out of fuel just shy of cutting through the last sheet of metal. Fresh debris meant this section of city was even less stable than they'd figured. If it was bad enough to send Beau forging an alternate route, that meant getting out through crumbling suburbs and shattered streets would be an arduous task at best.

He considered for a moment, then yanked his thick work gloves off and added them to the pile of equipment. He could complete the job when Beau returned. There was more fuel in the back of the truck, enough to let him finish cutting. This was a smaller haul than their last, but it would have to do. Riggs prayed it would be enough to barter, assuming he and Beau could find their way out of the dead city and back to what passed for civilization.

His long leather jacket also lay on the ground, the brown fabric contrasting starkly with the crumbled gray pavement beneath it. Riggs was tempted to shed one more layer, down to the thin T-shirt clinging to his sweat-slick skin, but he resisted the urge. For all that he was uncomfortably warm from his work, the chilly air made it a bad idea.

The growl of an approaching truck drew his attention, and he leaned down to fish the loaded revolver from the pocket of his coat. There was no mistaking the sound of that engine, but he clicked off the safety just the same. Always brace for the worst. It was a good philosophy for staying alive in a world gone wrong.

He didn't put the gun away until Beau had backed the enormous pickup right up to the ready pile of scrap and hopped out of the cab. For all that Riggs had been doing the heavier work in his absence, Beau was just as bedraggled. His dark hair looked nearly black, wet and plastered to his neck and cheeks, and his narrow face was gaunt in a way that said Riggs had better plan to cook up a little extra when they stopped for supper tonight. Beau wore a smile, but the expression was too tight to herald success.

"You didn't find any gasoline." Riggs tugged his gloves back on as he moved to unlock the tailgate.

Beau's smile faded and he shook his head. "I checked seven stations, three parking garages, and a car dealership. This place is tapped out. I found some kerosene and a stash of non-perishables, and I grabbed some fresh clothes while I was at it. But no fuel for the truck."

"We haven't run out yet." Riggs dropped the truck's lower gate with a thud, then propped the upper securely open. "We've got plenty to reach Almstead. We'll just have to trade for more when we get there." The prospect wasn't ideal. Food and gasoline were the two steepest commodities to barter for in this crude but functional economy. Workable metal only offered so much value, and he and Beau had little else to trade. This wasn't the first time things would be tight, but repetition didn't make the uncertainty any more appealing.

They would manage somehow.

"Come on." Riggs moved for the first pile of metal, each piece already cut down to fit the space available in the covered truck bed.

"Let's load this scrap and get the hell out of here."

"That's what I love about you, Riggs." Beau tugged his own thick gloves on as he approached the opposite edge of the pile. "You really know how to have fun."

Riggs only glared.

They worked efficiently, but it was still more than two hours before they finished loading, cutting down the last couple scraps, and locking their equipment securely in the truck alongside the fresh haul. Riggs shrugged back into his coat. He stifled an exhausted groan as he climbed into the driver's seat and slammed the door behind him.

Beau leveled a knowing look and slipped in through the opposite door, settling in on the passenger side of the worn bench seat.

"Fine. Next time *I'll* cut the scrap and *you* can fail at scavenging." Beau's expression was bland, but there was a hint of challenge in his voice.

Riggs snorted and turned the key in the ignition, gunning the pickup to life. The gas gauge had been broken for months, but he knew there was enough fuel in the tank to get them to the nearest bend in the river. They could stop there to refill from the gas can in back. The river bend was familiar ground sandwiched between pieces of nowhere. It would be relatively safe, with good cover for a night's rest.

The sun was beginning to sink, but assuming they could find a way out of here, they should make good time. Beau rolled down the window despite the clinging dust of dead city all around them. Riggs threw him a quick glance and then did the same.

*

Beau Greer had only been thirteen when the Vrete reached Earth. That was old enough to feel a choked foreboding right from the very first newscast, but still too young to be sure *why* he was afraid. His younger siblings were all giddy excitement watching the news coverage—a thousand spacecraft setting down in vacant fields all across the globe, gray-skinned figures emerging, looking not the slightest bit human as they sang their messages of peace.

Maybe they really had come in peace; it sucked that no one would ever know. The Vrete had come to emigrate, to share with humanity. They could help each other, claimed the many spokespeople. But when the human governments banded together to refuse, a more candid truth came out: now that they were here, the Vrete couldn't leave. Their ships were not equipped to depart again. They were here to stay, whether Earth accepted them or not.

Of course it was war after that. Whatever peace the Vrete had hoped to establish, there was no room in the human psyche for compromise.

The four years that followed were the worst flavors of Hell. By stubbornness and sheer numbers, humanity resisted an armada of superior technology, but it was never enough. Beau hadn't been old enough to enlist, but he didn't let that stop him. He was a good liar. He might not qualify for combat—there was no hiding his small stature or lack of training—but he landed in the medical corps and did plenty of good that way. It gave him someplace to belong when his hometown was incinerated in the backlash from an explosion meant for a bigger city. The medical corps gave him useful skills and a chance to save lives instead of taking them. It took Beau a while to appreciate these things, but by the end of the war he knew how lucky he was.

He was seventeen when humanity's final Hail Mary put a permanent stop to the fighting.

It wasn't a victory. It was a last, desperate offensive. A decision, by whatever powers still had the resources to decide, that they couldn't win. And if humanity couldn't keep this world, then damned if anyone else was going to take it. After four years of fighting, scientists had learned plenty about Vrete biology. They had identified the similarities, and the differences, between both contending species. They'd unlocked all the reasons Earth seemed such a promising prospect.

They had learned just what it would take to turn this promising world into an uninhabitable waste for the intruders intent on subsuming it.

They never considered peace instead.

Beau only ever knew the scant public details about that final offensive. There were rumors something big was coming, one decisive master stroke. Tangible hope, for the first time in four years of fighting. Then, so quickly no one understood at first, the cataclysm. Biological agents were introduced to alter the basic makeup of atmosphere, soil, water. The changes triggered a chain reaction that devastated the globe in less than a week. Nearly everyone, Beau included, thought it must've been an attack from the enemy.

Then the Vrete began to fall. By the hundreds. By the thousands. Until there were none left at all.

Mankind wasn't immune to the devastation. More than half of Earth's remaining population died in that first week, and the death toll tapered off only slowly in the months that followed. The modified atmosphere wasn't truly poisonous to humans, not the way it had been to the Vrete, but fewer people adapted than even the most cynical scientists could have predicted. The world changed, a harsh and fundamental shift. When the dust and blood had settled, countless species of plant and animal life were gone forever, and it was clear an irreparable wrong had been done.

What resources remained were funneled in a single direction. Enormous ships were built following the desperate blueprint of Vrete technology. A fleet of them, Cryo vessels that couldn't hope to hold even the diminished population still struggling to live on a poisoned world. In the end, those ships took only the children, along with the scant crew necessary to operate flight and settlement procedures. Beau Greer was seventeen. He had survived the violence of war and the changing Earth, but he was too old to escape on one of those ships.

The truth was, he'd been glad. There was too much ugly irony in that kind of escape, and even with all his imagination he couldn't picture a better future elsewhere.

He probably knew people on those ships, but he'd watched them take off with only a disconnected feeling of confusion. If any of his siblings were still alive, all but his sister would've been young enough to board. His own existence had already narrowed to surviving and doing whatever good he could manage. He never did learn if his family had survived the destruction of their hometown, and he would probably never know. He couldn't afford to wonder over questions without answers.

Once the war was over, Beau fell through the cracks. There was no more army, and the people who wanted him around weren't people he wanted much to do with. Better to keep his own company, to scavenge and survive with no one depending on him, and for a long time that's exactly what he did.

Beau's path crossed with Donovan Riggs three years after the end of the war. He met the man purely by accident, and wouldn't have collided with him at all if Beau weren't hungry and desperate. Beau wasn't usually a thief, but the night he met Riggs he was plain out of options. He hadn't intended to take much. Just some food, enough to get him to the next encampment past the river. But Riggs had caught him and knocked him flat on his back, almost breaking Beau's arm.

It was a little embarrassing how easily Riggs overpowered him. If Beau had been up to serious trouble—if he'd been carrying a weapon—he might not have lived to see the morning.

It wasn't until after stuttered apologies and tentative release that Beau had realized

Riggs was already injured, never mind how easily he'd won their altercation. From the way blood soaked through the fabric binding his thigh, he must've been hurt well before Beau snuck into the well-hidden campsite.

Beau made the offer without thinking. "I could stitch up that leg."

The look Riggs gave him was incredulous, the expression almost comic in the firelight, but he'd handed over what passed for his first aid kit and sat quietly through Beau's work.

Riggs looked a lot less terrifying in the light of the following morning. Handsome and wary, even if he could break Beau in half just as easily in the daylight. His silver hair was cropped severely short, and he carried himself with easy confidence despite the newly stitched injury. If Beau hadn't known better, he might've mistaken Riggs for ex-military, but there was something in his demeanor that didn't line up. Beau had worked with plenty of military types during the war, and Donovan Riggs wasn't quite like any of them, for all that Beau couldn't put his finger on *why.*

Riggs hadn't invited Beau along when he gathered his things, but he also hadn't protested when Beau hoisted his own pack and followed half a step behind.

After two years and counting, they were a team, and there was no going back.

*

"Hey." Beau reached across the seat to nudge Riggs in the arm, then pointed ahead and to the right. "You see that?" Down off the edge of the solid dirt path they were driving on, there was definitely something—maybe someone— slumped in the ditch.

"I see it." Riggs angled the truck as near that direction as possible without steering the tires off of firm ground.

Definitely some*one*, Beau decided as they drew closer. A person in dull clothes, curled forward on the muddy ground, impossible to distinguish in any detail. Beau grabbed the rifle from beneath his seat before they got close enough to see more. This area was mostly flat and clear, not many places to hide, but that didn't mean it *wasn't* some kind of ambush.

Riggs killed the engine a short ways from the slumped form and drew his favored revolver from the deep pocket of his coat. His face was guarded but not alarmed. His expression held only familiar alertness, and his every movement was cautious as he opened the driver's side door and stepped down. He locked the door behind him and waited while Beau did the same.

"Cover me," Riggs murmured when they met by the front bumper, still several feet from the figure in the ditch. "Keep close, but not too close. Stay alert."

Beau resisted the urge to roll his eyes. This wasn't the first wounded stranger Riggs had pulled over for, and it wouldn't even be the first to go poorly, if that was the turn things took. He split his attention between Riggs and the horizon as he followed a few steps behind, rifle at the ready and footsteps careful on the steep ground. He was glad the weather had been relatively dry, or the way would've been even more precarious. As it was, Beau still had to focus more than he'd like on his footing. Every second he spent with his attention on the ground made his heart beat faster.

They were still alone when they reached the figure in the scrubby foliage. It was a man, still breathing, though he gave no sign of noticing their approach. When Riggs tucked his weapon away and touched the man's shoulder, the only reaction it earned was a twitch and a muffled curse.

Riggs glanced up briefly, and Beau raised the rifle, sighted down the barrel as Riggs took a firmer grip on the man's shoulder. If the stranger planned to come up shooting, it would be on Beau to put him down before he could do any damage.

A gentle tug pulled the stranger back from his slump and settled him face-up against the slanting earth. No weapon came visible, and the man made an agonized sound at the movement. Beau could see why. Half his face was a pulp. Beneath the gray coat, his shirt was stained dark with too much blood. One good eye—dull green and wary—darted between Riggs and Beau. He was clearly aware of his surroundings despite being in obvious pain.

"Lea'mme 'lone," the wounded man rasped. Then, in a voice turned stronger by ferocious will, "Ain't got nothin' left to take."

"We're not here to steal from you." Riggs's voice was kinder than Beau had ever heard it. In two years, he'd never seen Riggs talk to a man who was so clearly dying. At least, not one who hadn't been aiming to cause trouble in the first place. He wasn't surprised Riggs didn't ask what happened. The man's words, not to mention his current condition, painted a clear enough picture. There was a reason, even with a truck and an impressive arsenal, Riggs always insisted on every caution. Beau was surprised when Riggs asked, "What's your name?"

The open green eye blinked, bleakly skeptical, but the man answered, "Garrett. Andrew Garrett." Then, in a voice heavy with hurt, "Ya got any water?"

Riggs threw a look to Beau, and Beau set aside his weapon to draw instead the canteen he always carried at his hip. He moved closer, knelt beside the man— Garrett—and twisted off the cap. He tried to hand the canteen over, but Garrett couldn't raise a hand to accept it, so Beau held it for him, tilting it to drip the water directly into his mouth.

"Can you help him?" Riggs asked. He was still looking at Garrett, but the question was for Beau.

Beau choked back the urge to snap that no, clearly there was nothing he could do.

Hell, he hadn't gotten a good look yet; maybe Garrett wasn't hurt as badly as he seemed. Beau set both canteen and rifle carefully aside, then reached for the blood-slick front of Garrett's shirt. A necklace tumbled free as he undid the top buttons, a tarnished crucifix on a rawhide strap. Beau ignored it in favor of the task at hand.

One look removed any doubt Beau might've held. Garrett's chest was a ruin, buckshot and bullet holes that hadn't been visible through the sodden pulp of the shirt. Only practice kept Beau's expression blank as he turned to Riggs and said, "I'm sorry." It seemed a wonder Garrett was still breathing now. Even if Beau had better than rudimentary tools to work with, he couldn't have saved this man. Beau was no surgeon, and whatever the magnitude of the external damage, he knew just how much worse it must be inside.

Beau offered more water, the only comfort he could give.

"You're Catholic?" Riggs asked Garrett, meeting his good eye with stern sympathy.

Garrett gave a wet, pained chuckle, then grimaced as the movement jarred his many hurts. "For all the good it'll do me," he muttered. "Ain't exactly a world of priests lining up to take m' confession."

"I can hear your confession," said Riggs.

Beau's head snapped up hard and fast, but Riggs barely spared him a glance before turning again to the man dying on the ground between them.

"Do you want me to administer last rites?" Riggs continued, as though he hadn't just been interrupted by Beau's silent surprise.

Garrett's good eye was open wide now, something like hope in its fading focus. "Please, Father."

Without looking away from Garrett's face, Riggs said, "Beau, go wait by the truck. This is private."

Beau hesitated a moment, but there was no defying a command like that. He re-capped the canteen and picked his rifle up from the muddy ground. He stayed vigilant as he climbed back up the ditch to the truck.

Privacy didn't mean he couldn't keep an eye on the proceedings.

Beau couldn't hear a word from his place by the pickup, but Garrett talked for a long time—longer than Beau would've thought he had the strength for—before tapering to exhausted silence. Riggs laid a steady hand over Garrett's forehead, and his entire face held an unfamiliar calm as he spoke words Beau couldn't decipher. Eventually Riggs stopped, too. There was a moment of perfect stillness, and then Riggs closed Garrett's eyes and murmured some final benediction.

It was several long minutes before Riggs rose to his feet and joined Beau on level ground. The lines of his face still held the same strange calm, but there was something cagey in his eyes.

"You're a priest." Beau meant it to be a question, but it didn't come out that way. Somehow he knew without any doubt that Riggs hadn't lied to comfort a dying man.

"I *was* a priest." Riggs slipped his revolver out of sight and moved toward the back of the truck with both hands free. Beau followed a step behind.

"But... a *priest.*"

Riggs stopped beside the rear tire, about-facing so suddenly that Beau had to brake hard not to trip over him. Beau froze too close, and for several seconds all he could do was blink up into Riggs's heavy stare. He was pretty sure he needed to find something more useful to say, but his voice stuck fast in his throat. From this close, Riggs's eyes were alarmingly blue.

Eventually, Riggs spoke without taking so much as a backward step. His voice, controlled at the best of times, was disconcertingly soft. "I haven't been a priest for a long time."

Beau swallowed past a throat gone tight. "Then what was all this?"

Riggs glanced past Beau, down the ravine. "Some things you don't get to turn your back on. No matter how much you might quit." Then he turned and rounded the bed of the truck, all business. "Come on. Let's bury this poor bastard and get back on the road."

*

Riggs still felt rattled the next day, distracted no matter how firmly he tried to keep his mind on their route. He had managed to go a hell of a long time without thinking about the Church. Suddenly he could think of little else.

Before the Vrete, Riggs's faith had been potent. He'd been a poor preacher even then—too brusque for eloquent homilies, too pragmatic for his strictest vows—but his heart had always been in the right place. He'd been a man who knew just where he belonged, who understood his world and his own place in it.

Then the war came, a calamity like humanity had never seen. It broke the world and took away everything that mattered. A contest four awful years in the fighting.

Donovan Riggs had given up on God by the end of year one.

He hadn't openly forsaken his calling until well after the fighting stopped. Riggs was a damn good liar, as it turned out. Humanity needed men of faith to stand behind them through bad and worse, and Riggs was determined to do his part even if he had to pretend every step of the way. He had always suspected he wasn't the only priest playing that game.

By the time mankind had Earth to itself again, there hadn't been enough left of the Catholic Church for Riggs to formally resign. He'd simply dropped the act, along with everything else about his life before, and focused on learning to live in what was left of the world.

He shook himself out of his own sour headspace when the outskirts of Almstead finally rose ahead. 'Outskirts' was a misleading term. Most of the community was just as raw as the homesteads that formed a rough perimeter around the sturdier central buildings. There were walls edging most of the fields, and despite the toxic soil, sullen plant life grew in meticulous rows. It was agriculture, or near enough. For all his cynicism, Riggs had to concede the sight was impressive. He and Beau would be trading for some of those foodstuffs today, along with a dozen other things they couldn't scavenge for themselves.

Rather than navigate between the fields, Riggs angled the pickup to circle the periphery. Within fifteen minutes he was parking in a familiar clearing, just inside the westernmost fields. There were a handful of other vehicles already there. A couple were local, but most were visitors here to trade.

Plenty of townsfolk milled about, talking to anyone with stock to barter.

Riggs gestured at Beau to leave his rifle beneath the seat. They'd never had that kind of trouble here, though Riggs kept his own weapon in his pocket just the same. It didn't pay to be careless.

They traded nearly all their scrap for food, ammo, and gasoline. There was plenty of use for metal in a town like this, but the lot still didn't take them as far as he'd hoped. Their final customer offered a better deal than she probably should have, and it wasn't difficult to tell why. It would've been tough to mistake the way she hovered in Riggs's space while they discussed terms.

She was an attractive woman, with a thickset figure and a pretty smile. She smelled nice. Riggs found himself smiling back without consciously meaning to. That it seemed to have done them some good by way of negotiation was a bonus he didn't consider until she was carrying her goods away on a low cart.

Beau's voice in his ear startled him, but not enough that Riggs let his reaction show. "You sly silver fox." There was laughter in the words, and unmistakable fondness.

It took conscious effort, but Riggs managed a stern expression when he turned to look Beau in the eye. "Don't call me that."

Beau only grinned wider, and followed him back to the truck.

They made camp late that night, after putting several hours' distance between themselves and Almstead. The stop was a solid stretch of miles toward their next scavenging target, but they still had a good distance to travel. Dinner cooked over a small campfire was uninspired, but for once it was fresh, a tumble of stringy vegetables thrown together mostly at random. Beau complained of burnt edges, just like always.

To date he had never volunteered to do the cooking himself.

It was Beau who put the fire out, but with obvious reluctance. Bitter wind cut through their camp, despite the steep walls of dirt to either side. The air was cold enough that Riggs considered gathering the insulated tent from the truck and setting it up in the dark. The warmth wasn't quite worth the tradeoff in mobility, though. Not yet. Not for another month, maybe, if the weather held. For now it was better to be out in the relative open, where the slightest sound would alert them instantly to trouble.

Riggs burrowed into his side of the bedroll, shifting beneath heavy covers and making sure his revolver was in reach where it belonged. Beau settled in behind him, muttering curses about the wind and already doing his best to snag more than his share of the covers. Riggs waited through an extra moment's restlessness as Beau checked his own weapon, but eventually there was only stillness and wind, and the grudging warmth of shared body heat.

They always slept back-to-back. Even on warmer nights it was force of habit. Safer. Harder for anyone to catch them off guard this way, when both Riggs and Beau were light sleepers and had each other's backs.

There was something reassuring in having Beau so close, though Riggs would never admit it. Fierce protectiveness lodged in his chest, even if he still wasn't sure how Beau had become so vital to him. Being able to hear the steady in-and-out of Beau breathing in the dark calmed him in a way Riggs didn't bother trying to explain.

He thought Beau was already asleep, so he started when Beau's voice cut through the quiet.

"We could be sleeping inside actual walls right now."

"How d'you figure?" Riggs blinked into the gritty darkness.

"The woman at Almstead? You know, our last customer? The one who couldn't stop ogling you?"

"What about her?" Riggs already knew where Beau was going with this, but he kept his tone bland anyway. Being curt never actually dissuaded Beau from making a point.

"Just seems like she'd have been pleased if you decided to stay."

"Why on earth would I stay?" When the first hint of irritation leaked into his words, Riggs did nothing to temper his tone.

"Dunno." The carelessness in Beau's voice was too deliberate. They'd argued through too many variations on this conversation. It had nothing at all to do with Riggs's love life, and everything to do with the constant wandering he and Beau lived by. He wondered if Beau thought he was being subtle, asking questions that made it clear how much he wanted to stay, every time they skirted a place where some optimistic idiot had put down roots.

Tonight Riggs didn't feel like arguing over the fact that there was no point. Sure, in the short term it was nice to know there were people who could cultivate a food supply. It was useful as hell having someone to trade with, and he wasn't going to try and talk anyone out of a stationary lifestyle. Riggs wasn't the only one with a stubborn need to survive. Much as he wasn't generally fond of people, he also knew he couldn't win every battle alone.

But building up from nothing, the way some had started to do—settling and striving and trying to carve something more permanent out of a busted landscape—Riggs couldn't fathom it. Why build something to last when you had no one to pass it on to? The war had been over for five years. In all that time, Riggs had never seen a single child. There had been no pregnancies, no babies, *nothing.* He was no scientist to analyze why, but it didn't take much to figure it had something to do with the lingering damage to air and soil.

"*You* could have stayed," Riggs said, though the idea stuck unpleasantly in his chest. If Beau did decide to stay at one of the communities they traded with, Riggs wouldn't try to stop him. But he damn well wouldn't like it.

"Nah." Beau's voice was heavy—whether with sleep or meaning—but something about it slid beneath Riggs's skin and settled nerves he hadn't even realized were riled. "I'd rather stick with you."

"Guess you're smarter than you look." It was a transparent attempt to lighten the air, but Beau chuckled anyway.

"Just because I'm beautiful doesn't mean I can't be brilliant." Beau shifted behind him now, fitting more snugly along Riggs's back. When he spoke again, the momentary levity had bled from his voice. "Don't you ever think it might be nice, though? Stick around somewhere long enough to learn people's names, sleep in a bed, build a roof to keep the rain off... Have an actual *home*, you know?"

An old, exhausted yearning gnawed at Riggs with the question, followed by anger, and then a moment later by dull resignation. His voice, when he answered, was cold even to his own ears.

"There's no such thing."

*

The ruined vestiges of Des Moines were still two days out when the sun began to sink low. They had at least an hour of good driving light, but Beau started looking for a decent stopover anyway. They'd already been navigating for eight hours, over flat ground and crumbled highways, and also several long stretches of nastier terrain that made the entire truck lurch and rattle.

Even here the lower ground was all muck and mud, but there were plenty of higher hills, and some weak patches of bush and timber that promised to keep them out of sight. Many of the trees were dead, some fallen, some still upright amid hardier specimens with leaves of brown and red.

One tree in particular caught Beau's eye as he pulled into a clearing between three separate copses. The oak was tall and huge, bigger by far than any of the others nearby. From the bare limbs and the pale, twisted look of its trunk, it had been dead for a long time. A hard gust of wind blew, shaking leaves and branches all around the clearing, and the massive tree quivered in a way that was far from reassuring.

Beau parked the truck at a safe distance, and he and Riggs worked in silence, gathering wood and setting up their minimal camp. One thing Beau had learned in the past two years: when Riggs wasn't in the mood to chat, there was no point pressing him.

A shiver of unexplained trepidation ran the length of Beau's spine just as he dropped a heavy bundle of bedding. He froze and sought Riggs with his eyes. Riggs was already tensing into a crouch, slipping a hand into the pocket where he kept his gun. Beau's chest tightened, and he reached for the rifle that was never far from hand, just in time to hear the snap of a branch behind him.

Instinct sent him to the ground hard and fast, already twisting to look as a deafening report of gunfire cracked from the same direction. A bullet kicked up a spray of dirt too close for comfort, and Beau scrambled away from the pickup, toward the nearest trees. There was more gunfire, Riggs shooting into the scrubby foliage. More bullets zinged too close as Beau scrambled for cover. He shouted at Riggs, all adrenaline and exasperation, and finally Riggs moved, dodging out of sight.

Beau couldn't tell exactly how many people were closing in. Whoever they were, they were maneuvering behind the limited trees, half a dozen people at least, maybe more. Beau tried to keep watch in all directions at once, even behind lest someone circle around to flank him. From behind his own chosen tree trunk, he raised his rifle, searching for a target.

He couldn't find a single clear shot.

Somewhere to his right, he heard the bang of Riggs's revolver. From the foliage straight ahead came a quickly strangled scream as one of their assailants crumpled forward from hiding. Dead. Or dying so fast it barely mattered.

Beau scanned the spaces between trees and managed to put a bullet through an exposed shoulder across the clearing. His ears were ringing too loudly to tell if his target screamed on being hit.

He didn't manage to take anyone else down, though Riggs put a bullet in at least one more stranger before reloading the revolver. There was no way out of this. They were too badly outnumbered. The damage Beau and Riggs had managed to inflict was nowhere near enough.

Once they were surrounded, it was painfully clear that they'd never stood a chance.

There were nine combatants still standing, six men and three women by Beau's count, all tough and raw. None of them bothered to hide their faces as they emerged into the open. All held weapons at the ready, three guns aiming at Beau from close range, the rest trained on Riggs.

"This is *shit*," Beau snarled. Fear and anger twisted his insides as he set his still-loaded rifle on the ground by his knees. In his peripheral vision, he could see Riggs doing the same with his revolver, but Beau didn't dare take his eyes off the closest muzzles staring him in the face. He didn't need a clear look to recognize the furious tension in Riggs's shoulders anyway. He didn't need to *see* to sense anger in the air, rage to match his own.

The man standing nearest Beau had a weasel's face and a head of patchy hair that clearly hadn't been washed in recent memory. When he took a step closer, Beau could smell him, and his stomach did an unpleasant flop.

The man held out a skinny hand, palm up, and said, "Keys."

Beau glared, unmoving, despite the fact that the man's other hand still held a gun aimed straight at his head.

The man threw an irritated look at one of his companions, then turned a harder stare on Beau. "If you give us the keys to your truck and walk away, we'll let you leave in one piece."

Beau's jaw clenched, and he could feel Riggs's eyes on him now. Even if they had any hope of surviving without the supplies in that truck, he knew they weren't walking out of this clearing alive. Plenty of people had an easier time shooting a man in the back than in the face. Weasel here seemed just that kind of coward.

Beau had no intention of giving these assholes the satisfaction.

For an instant, when he heard the fresh gunshot, he was certain he'd been killed and just hadn't felt it yet. It took him maybe a tenth of a second to realize Weasel-face *hadn't* fired—that the weasel was *dropping his weapon*, was falling to his knees with a wounded curse—and then Beau moved on nothing but instinct. He grabbed for his rifle and ducked for deeper cover in the thin patch of trees, as their eight remaining assailants shouted and scattered. Another two went down to the sound of a shotgun discharging twice in quick succession. Beau searched the tree line, confused and frantic. A spot of deep red caught his attention. It wasn't blood, he realized, but a woman in a brown jacket with a dark red shirt. She cast aside her weapon and dove for the man trying to escape past her.

She was a tall woman, broad and muscular, and she took her target down hard. She was barely bigger than him, but she knocked his gun away, then managed with her fists in the absence of a weapon.

Beau's attention twitched just in time to raise his own gun and take down another fleeing target—a skinny woman with pale hair—before she could reach the far side of the clearing. Beside her, a shot from Riggs's revolver dropped another of their attackers. That should have left three, but there was one body too many on the ground, and only two figures now trying to retreat.

Two more strangers stepped out from between the trees, each with a gun trained on one of the fleeing assailants. One of the newcomers was a tiny woman with short black hair, carrying a heavy shotgun like she didn't notice the weight. The other was a tall man, surely no older than Beau and easily the skinniest person Beau had ever seen, cupping a smaller firearm with both hands. Beau stared, incredulous, as Shotgun took calm aim and blew the head off the runner just reaching the trees. Her entire body kicked with the recoil, but she held her ground with practiced ease. Skinny fired at the nearer, final straggler, but caught him in the shoulder instead of a killing blow. Shotgun stepped calmly forward and finished the job.

It was over so quickly Beau's head spun. Across the clearing, Red was only now rising to her feet, leaving her opponent unmoving on the ground.

"Everybody in one piece?" Shotgun shouted. She was nudging one of the fallen bodies with a distasteful toe, checking to be sure it was dead.

"Who the hell are you people?" Riggs called instead of answering. Beau recognized wary disbelief in his voice, but he was confident Riggs would hear their rescuers out.

Beau kept his own weapon at the ready, held steadily in both hands as he rose to his feet. He emerged cautiously around the thick tree trunk, towards the converging strangers. All three were behaving much the same. They carried weapons in hand—Red had reclaimed hers from the ground—but weren't raising them or taking aim. There was nothing threatening in their movements.

The situation was delicate, but maybe it didn't have to be deadly. Beau just needed to keep Riggs from shooting anyone and pray this lot wasn't after their truck and wares for themselves.

The last thing Beau expected to hear in that moment was the mounting roar of an engine gunning nearby. He swiveled his head in the direction of the sound, just in time to see a black jeep tear into the clearing, grinding mud and fallen wood beneath its enormous wheels. There was one man inside. He held the steering wheel with one hand, a gun in the other, and he was aiming the weapon straight out the window.

"*Riggs!*" Beau dropped his rifle and dove, throwing himself forward. He collided hard, taking them both down just as the man in the jeep pulled the trigger. The bullet grazed so close it clipped the collar of Beau's coat.

They hit the ground with a jolt behind the tallest tree. Riggs landed hard on his back, probably hitting his head on the wide-sprawling roots. Beau landed awkwardly astride him, already contorting for a glimpse around the dead trunk. He saw Shotgun drop her spent weapon and draw a handgun from the small of her back. She didn't flinch from the sound of another returning gunshot, though her two companions scrambled for cover. Red and Skinny clearly had all the sense of that bunch. Shotgun simply sighted down the length of the handgun, taking steady aim, and calmly pulled the trigger. Her shot went through the windshield, spider-webbing the glass and spattering blood through the open passenger window.

Beau stared, expecting the jeep to slow. Even if the driver wasn't dead, surely he was hurt badly. But the vehicle was coming straight for them now. If anything it sped up, plowing with a shudder into the massive trunk of the dead tree sheltering Beau and Riggs.

The tree gave a groan, a creaky wobble, then began to fall. Straight towards them.

From the other side of the tree, Shotgun's shrill voice called, "Look out!"

This time it was Riggs who moved with startling speed. His hands closed hard on Beau, grasping him soundly as Riggs threw his weight and rolled them to the side, just barely out of the path of the falling trunk. There wasn't time to retreat farther, but Riggs's body curled down, a protective shield pinning Beau to the ground. An avalanche of branches crashed on top of them, snapping and splintering and twisting against the earth. Beau's fingers twisted in the front of Riggs's shirt, and he felt powerful arms close around him, crushing him and squeezing the air out of his lungs.

In the stillness after, it took several seconds for Riggs to shift and loosen his bruising hold. Beau let go his own grip with difficulty. Riggs's worried face hovered close above him, peering down with sharp concern.

"Are you all right?" Riggs's question was quiet gravel, and Beau became abruptly aware of the thoughtless tangle of their limbs. The weight on top of him was distracting as hell, firm muscle keeping

Beau pinned even now that the danger had passed.

Beau swallowed and retorted, "Are *you*?"

"You boys coming out from under there any time this decade?" called a low alto voice from the clearing.

Riggs finally rose to his hands and knees so that Beau could crawl out from beneath the broken mess of branches that had come down atop them. Riggs followed close behind, picking up his revolver along the way and dusting dirt from his clothes.

Beau watched him with a medic's eye. Riggs was moving gingerly, but not so carefully that Beau figured the tree had done him serious harm. He didn't dare pause to ask now. There could still be danger lurking out of sight.

But by the time Beau had reclaimed his rifle from the ground, he dared to hope that no more company was coming. Their three rescuers stood a good distance from the felled tree and crumpled jeep. They were near—though not too near—Riggs and Beau's locked truck. The woman in the red shirt, almost certainly the owner of the voice that had called them a moment ago, had dark skin and kind eyes.

"The idiot in the jeep must've been all the cavalry they had," she said, confirming Beau's theory.

"Who are you people?" Riggs repeated his earlier question. His voice was calm now that they weren't surrounded by weapons fire. Instead of looking offended, Red smirked and glanced at her smaller-statured companion.

It was Shotgun who stepped forward, tucking her handgun out of sight in order to extend a hand in greeting. She still held the shotgun in her other grip, but there was nothing actively threatening in the casual way she carried the weapon.

"Yuko Han," she said. Sensing Riggs's hesitation, Beau intercepted the handshake enthusiastically. When she dropped his hand, it was to point at Red and Skinny, and announce, "Mel. And Sammy."

"Beau," he offered in return. He nodded at his partner and added, "Donovan Riggs."

"You two are damn lucky." Yuko's eyes darted between them, but her demeanor was unhurried. Beau was starting to believe these three were no more trouble than they seemed. "If we hadn't been near enough to hear gunfire, you'd probably be dead right now."

"We'd have managed," Riggs said.

Beau elbowed him in the side. "He means 'thank you'."

"Don't worry," Yuko said with a wry smile. "I speak fluent curmudgeon."

Beau stifled a snort as Riggs edged in front of him—goddamn overprotective cowboy—and then Riggs asked, "What's the catch?"

The silence that followed was more considering than awkward, all three newcomers exchanging eloquent looks. When they had come to some wordless consensus, it was Mel who spoke.

"Be reasonable to spot us some ammo, considering we just spent our own to save your tails. But besides that, it's up to your conscience."

Beau knew his first instinct, inviting them to stick around and share supper, wouldn't fly. It simply wasn't safe to stay here. The idiot in the jeep might not have been the only cavalry—he might just have been the closest. So without giving Riggs a chance to protest, Beau unlocked the truck bed and packed a cloth sack with what ammo and foodstuffs they could afford to part with.

There was a new bullet hole in the side of the pickup, positioned alarmingly close to the gallons of spare gasoline. They were damn lucky to still have a vehicle.

"Don't take this the wrong way," Beau said, handing the bag of supplies over to the trio that had just saved their asses, "but we'll let you leave first." Beside him, Riggs gave a small but approving nod. Yuko's answering smile was knowing, as was the amused look she exchanged with Mel.

"Cautious. Fair enough."

It wasn't until the three were well out of sight that Beau turned to look directly at Riggs. Only then did he notice the wide rip in Riggs's sleeve, and the blood that had dripped down his arm to paint his hand red at his side.

"You asshole, why didn't you say you were hurt?" Beau set his rifle down and leaned close to inspect the gash. Riggs made an impatient sound, but he didn't pull away from Beau's inspection. After two years, he knew better.

The wound was still bleeding steadily, not so hard as to set Beau panicking, but hard enough he wasn't pleased to only be discovering it now. It was clearly a bullet wound, a deep graze, but it didn't seem to have hit anything vital.

"I'll need to stitch this up," Beau muttered.

"Later. We can't stay here. We need to move."

He was right, and Beau cursed as he darted back to the truck, fishing a clean cloth from the box of first aid supplies. He wound the cloth around Riggs's arm, cinching it tight.

"The second we stop for the night, you're letting me take care of that."

"Promise," Riggs agreed.

*

They didn't have much camp to pack up, and Beau slipped behind the wheel before Riggs could protest. He couldn't tell how much blood Riggs had lost, but Beau wouldn't put it past him to try and make a pissing match out of whose turn it was to drive.

Riggs didn't argue, though. He was subdued as he settled at the other end of the wide bench seat, staring straight out the windshield, his expression heavy.

Beau put the truck in gear and drove as fast as he dared, covering as much ground as he could before the last of the sun set. He had to slow down then for safety, but a full moon above meant he didn't have to risk using the headlights. He navigated cautiously, stuck to the clearest paths and the highest ground, until he found a natural gap between hills. It was the best location they were likely to find tonight, and he parked the truck with a lurch.

They'd have to risk a fire. He needed more than moonlight for stitching, but at least here the light wouldn't be visible at a distance.

They made camp quickly and carelessly, and despite his arm Riggs made a fire while Beau unrolled the small pack of supplies he would need. Riggs was moving even more gingerly now, and from the dark crease between his brows he was really starting to feel his open wound.

Beau watched Riggs untie the sodden cloth from around his arm and shrug painfully out of his jacket, then had to help tug the ruined shirt up and off. The bare lines of Riggs's chest cast strong shadows in the firelight—firm muscle and plenty of scars. To Beau's credit, it only took him a couple seconds to tear his eyes away and turn his attention to the task at hand.

"Here." He tossed Riggs a bottle of moonshine from their bags—vile stuff, but effective for more than one purpose. He watched Riggs knock back a generous swallow with a scowl at the taste, then snagged it back from him. "Steady on," Beau murmured, and without warning he poured the alcohol over the gash in Riggs's arm.

Riggs made no sound, but his whole body tensed at the sting. The muscles of his throat strained visibly with the effort of silence. The second Beau was finished, before he could recap the bottle, Riggs snagged it back and took another long swallow. He'd be loaded fast if he kept that up, but as long as he could sit still, Beau wouldn't protest.

He had no way to sterilize his hands, but he did have a box of clean rubber gloves, and

Beau tugged a pair on. He stitched efficiently, as quickly and carefully as he could, placing his sutures in an even row as Riggs stared into the fire.

Only after Beau secured a heavy bandage around his finished work did Riggs recap the bottle of rotgut and set it aside. Beau studied Riggs's fire-lit profile, the tired lines of Riggs's face, and did his best not to let his eyes wander. It wouldn't do to be caught ogling. That way lay more awkwardness than he was in the mood to cope with tonight.

"Better?" Beau asked. He was startled when Riggs turned and caught him with a fierce look, eyes far too sharp for the amount of alcohol Beau had watched him drink.

"Always," Riggs said. Then, still staring hard and speaking in a voice gone gruff, "You should be more careful."

Beau blinked at him, incredulous. "*I* should be more careful?"

"You almost took a bullet today, trying to save *my* neck. That's not a fair trade."

Anger sent a spike of cold along Beau's spine, set his heart racing in his chest. He could feel a fight coming—an argument that wouldn't do any damn good even if Riggs were sober—and it was only with enormous willpower that Beau kept his voice bland as he answered, "Who says you get to make that call?"

Bland or not, the words were still a deliberate goad, and Beau was surprised when Riggs failed to rise to the bait.

Riggs's eyes cut away, toward his unopened pack near the fire, and he reached to tug it closer, spent a silent moment digging inside for a clean shirt. Beau didn't offer to help him shrug into the fresh garment, or button it up the front, even when Riggs gave up with five buttons left to go and the collar hanging open. The silence stretched unsteadily between them, and several minutes passed before Riggs turned to face him.

The rough edge of his voice had turned confessional now, an uncomfortable honesty that made Beau's face heat and his heart pound. "I can't lose you, Beau. Haven't got anyone else left that's *mine.*"

Mine, he said. Like whatever kept them together, guarding each other's backs, was so basic and simple it could be summed up in that one word. It made Beau feel secure, *safe*, in a way he'd almost forgotten was possible. It also made him feel too exposed, and he smiled uncertainly.

"I don't think I've ever seen you this drunk before. Makes you almost charming."

But for all the forced lightness in Beau's tone, Riggs just held him in that too-intense stare. The smile, weak to begin with, fell from Beau's mouth in the quiet. He couldn't keep meeting Riggs's eyes, so he shifted where he sat and stared into the fire instead.

He realized belatedly that he was still wearing the bloodied gloves, and he tugged them off slowly, letting them turn inside out as he peeled them from his hands. He didn't dare raise his eyes again; he was too nervous about what Riggs might see.

"Those ships took away everything that mattered," Riggs said. He sounded distant now, and Beau risked a glance. He breathed easier when he realized Riggs *wasn't* looking at him anymore. Riggs was slouched forward, watching the flames.

Beau knew what Riggs was seeing: those cryo ships, the ones that took the children and what little hope Earth had left, and flew them into forever because there was nothing left for them here. Beau had been at the Kansas City shipyards, determined to see the launch for himself. Whether his brothers were on that monstrosity or not, Beau had needed to watch with his own eyes as the fleet rose into the sky. Every last child had been loaded aboard before liftoff. Deep down in his gut Beau had recognized the truth: those ships were taking the entire future with them, leaving only dust and ashes behind.

Riggs's voice was impossibly soft when he said, "They took my little girl."

Shock froze Beau, and suddenly he could barely hear the pop and crackle of the fire through the ringing in his ears. He'd thought Riggs must surely be out of surprises by now.

He didn't know why this revelation was so much more staggering than even the fact that Riggs was a priest, but it took Beau half an eternity to respond. "You had a daughter?"

"I *have* a daughter. Out there." Riggs was staring skyward now, and his voice held an edge that Beau knew not to argue with.

"But... you were a *priest.*" A Catholic priest, going by what Beau had witnessed on the road scant days past. Beau didn't fuck with religion much, but he knew *that* wasn't in the rulebook.

To Beau's surprise, the protest softened Riggs's expression and drew a pained chuckle from his throat. Several seconds passed, but eventually Riggs turned his head to peer at Beau slantwise. Firelight warmed the reluctant smile on his face.

"I never said I was a *good* priest."

It still took Beau several seconds to wrap his head around this new information, cryptic as it was. When he'd more or less managed the trick, he was surprised to hear himself ask, "Do you think they're all okay? The kids on those ships?"

"Of course they are." Again there was something unyielding in Riggs's eyes, a stubborn certainty that Beau ached to understand.

"How can you be sure?" he asked, his own voice achingly soft.

"Because," Riggs said without any hesitation at all, "they have to be."

*

They managed another heavy scavenge, this time from the garage of an abandoned airfield. No fuel to speak of, and certainly nothing else by way of useful supplies, but the metal they cut was cleaner and sturdier than their usual. Riggs was confident it would bring better trade than the last batch.

They were halfway to Joram when they stopped for the night. They settled in for uncomfortable sleep beside a small river that offered, if nothing else, the chance to bathe in its frigid water. The nights were getting cold enough that Beau had started hinting maybe it was time to put up the thermal tent, but Riggs didn't want to concede the readiness that came of bedding down in the open. He certainly didn't like the prospect so soon after their recent brush with violence. His arm ached, though the gash was healing quickly beneath Beau's careful stitches.

There was no telling if the wound would scar, but Riggs didn't particularly care. What was one more to add to the collection?

As they crawled beneath heavily layered blankets Riggs ignored a running commentary, except to note that Beau sounded tired as he muttered 'just saying' and 'fucking freezing out here' and 'couldn't we just'. There was the customary fidgeting as they settled back-to-back, the usual scuffle of sharing covers, and then stillness. Beau's sigh was almost imperceptible. More evident by far was the tired strain in his body, impossible for Riggs to ignore with Beau's back pressed warmly along his own.

Beau had been chewing on *something* for the past few days. Quiet was not a good look on him, but so far Riggs had resisted the urge to pry. Now, in cooling darkness with only moonlight ghosting down, he had to exercise deliberate restraint just to keep his mouth shut.

"Hey, Don," Beau said, and Riggs tensed with surprise. In two years, Beau had never used his first name. "Can I ask you something?"

"Sure." Riggs didn't have much success keeping the apprehension out of his voice.

"What are you looking for?"

There was an edge to the question. No idle curiosity, this, but the crux of whatever itch had stuck beneath Beau's skin all week. Defensiveness surged in Riggs's chest, and his guard rose at being asked something so shrewdly personal. Beau wasn't fishing, but Riggs couldn't bring himself to answer, either. He didn't have words for the phantom ache that kept him constantly on the move, dragging Beau along every step of the way.

"Who says I'm looking for anything?" he evaded. The hard edges of his revolver were muffled beneath the bundle that served as his pillow, and in the open moonlight he could see a good distance straight ahead.

Seconds dragged long, and instead of answering Beau moved, shifting clumsily to lie on his back. His arm pressed between Riggs's shoulder blades.

"What's your daughter's name?" Beau asked into the shuttered quiet.

Again Riggs froze, caught off guard. It took him several careful breaths before he managed to answer, "Amanda." Another thirty seconds passed before he heard his own rough voice say, "Why are you asking about this?"

Beau shrugged—Riggs felt the gesture against his back—but didn't answer aloud. The silence was jarring, as uncharacteristic as Beau's stubborn quiet over the past several days, and Riggs exhaled heavily. Despite the ache in his chest, he twisted beneath the blankets, maneuvering carefully in an attempt to keep cold air from sneaking in. He shifted onto his back and then the rest of the way over, up onto one elbow. The effort put pressure on his nearly healed arm, but not enough to dissuade him. It also put him far too close, but Beau didn't seem troubled by the proximity.

Riggs hesitated, peering down at Beau, trying without success to read his face in the watery moonlight.

When the silence drew so long it threatened to choke him, Riggs asked, "What the hell, Beau?"

"It's just... I didn't even know you *had* daughter. All this time we've been partners, and you never talked about her."

A frantic feeling too sharp to be laughter threatened in Riggs's chest. Of course he never talked about Amanda. He may have been a crap father when she was still here, but after five years her absence still hurt. Far too much to express with a jumble of inadequate words.

It was mostly defensive instinct that made Riggs glare down at Beau and counter, "You never talk about *your* family, either."

"I would if you asked," Beau said, not at all the answer Riggs expected. "If you wanted to know." The words held too much meaning, an offer and a challenge. Beau stared straight up at Riggs, unflinching determination and something more in his eyes. Something fierce and fond, and maybe a little bit hungry—something that had everything to do with the way Beau didn't even seem to notice Riggs leaning closer, practically on top of him—like this quiet intimacy was no surprise at all.

Something bright and keen clicked into place in Riggs's head, and he moved without thought. Instinct pulled him forward, and he leaned down, closing the distance between them and taking Beau's mouth in a sudden kiss.

Beau breathed a startled sound, but he didn't protest. By the time Riggs's brain caught up enough to send messages like *stop* and *panic* and *retreat*, Beau's fingers were twined tightly in the front of his shirt, holding fast and keeping him close.

It was an invitation Riggs would have to be made of stone to resist, and he dropped the rest of the way forward, letting his weight carry him down, blanketing Beau with the length of his body as he coaxed the kiss deeper. Beau's hands released his shirtfront to frame his face instead. Beau was maddening heat, restless and greedy and arching beneath Riggs, offering friction that threatened to overwhelm tenuous control.

It had been too goddamn long. Fleeting moments with his own right hand were better than nothing, but even those were few and far between. He and Beau lived too securely in each other's pockets. What little privacy existed between them was constantly dwindling. Riggs honestly couldn't remember the last time he'd had a few scattered moments to himself, which meant it had been months, maybe longer. No wonder he was already coming apart.

Riggs groaned, breaking free to press rough kisses beneath Beau's jaw. Frustration mounted beneath his skin. They both slept fully clothed, and there were too many layers between them. He could feel the stiffness of an erection to match his own as he slid one leg between Beau's thighs, and then he didn't have anywhere near enough brainpower to keep wishing they were both naked. Beau was twisting beneath him now, rubbing against him. They were kissing again, but all their coordination had evaporated. Beau's body was wiry strength in Riggs's arms, sure and solid and more demanding with every passing second.

They both came quietly—Riggs choking down a shout—Beau muffling his own sounds against Riggs's throat. No amount of passion could overwrite the danger of being heard, and they were both too practiced at caution to be careless now.

Groggy satisfaction made Riggs's limbs and eyelids heavy, but the lethargy only lasted a moment or two. Adrenaline followed fast on its heels, a sudden awareness of the body beneath him. He could feel the rise and fall of Beau's chest, the strength of Beau's arms holding him as their heartbeats settled in tandem.

Reluctantly, Riggs pressed up onto his elbows.

He found Beau watching him, dark heat banking in brown eyes. They were both still breathing hard, and in the stilted moments of *after* they gawped at each other with matching stares. Five seconds. Ten. Thirty seconds, and Riggs still couldn't speak. Even if he could, what would he possibly say?

Beau's expression shuttered, maybe in response to the confounded look Riggs couldn't seem to wipe off his own face. Neither of them said a word. The silence was too stubborn, the awkwardness impenetrable. It took Riggs what felt like an eternity to take his hands from Beau and climb off of him. All this he managed without leaving the disheveled pile of blankets, though he suddenly felt over-warm, not to mention uncomfortable and sticky in other ways.

Settling on his own half of the pallet— taking his customary place like nothing had just happened—was the coward's way out. But a winded tightness in Riggs's chest left him no better alternative. He couldn't wrap his head around what he'd just let himself do. He couldn't decipher where it had come from. The potency of his sudden need to touch surprised and terrified him, and he didn't like being caught off guard by something he should've recognized months ago.

Eventually he slept, while behind him Beau pretended to do the same.

*

They didn't talk about it come morning. Or during any of the days of travel that followed. A dozen times Beau tried to ease into the subject. He aimed for subtlety, because he suspected Riggs would spook if he approached too directly. He'd witnessed conversations not even half this awkward send Riggs into retreat. The man had no problem finding some task that needed doing just out of earshot, or even farther away, if it meant avoiding an unwelcome conversation.

All Beau's attempts predictably failed. As it turned out, there was no smooth way to bring up the fact that Riggs had kissed him and then some. The problem was, if he couldn't get Riggs to talk about it, he definitely had no hope Riggs would do it again.

Beau had already spent too long trying to keep his eyes and hands to himself. He refused to accept a world in which this was a one-time thing.

Riggs was stubborn. He wasn't talking. But he was *looking* now, in those distracted moments when he didn't expect Beau to be paying attention. He was watching more closely than he ever had before, and Beau did his damnedest not to let on how obvious he was being about it.

Beau played oblivious when he paused unloading equipment and caught Riggs staring at his ass. He pretended not to notice whenever Riggs's eyes lingered too long, because getting caught might make Riggs stop, which was the last thing Beau wanted.

They worked hard, same as always. They gathered subpar scrap from sludgy terrain and bartered it at Camp Reming, then moved on and did it again. Same gig, different settlement. There was something almost reassuring in the monotony of the work, or there would have been if it weren't for the simmering tension that hung between them like a tangible intruder.

Riggs wanted him. Nearly two weeks out, Beau was surer of this than ever. But they still weren't talking about it, and the greedy impatience in Beau's chest would drive him out of his mind if something didn't change.

The settling chill of autumn gave way unexpectedly to heat, bringing heavy storm clouds that hung over the flat horizon like a taunt. Beau and Riggs worked only in shirt sleeves during those three suffocating days, stopping well before dusk on the final afternoon.

"Trust me," Beau insisted. He had a nose for weather, and he could feel it in the air, the threat of storm looming heavier than ever. "We don't want to be out in the open much longer."

The sky should have been a bruised gray at this hour, but instead the clouds clung greenish yellow. Beau and Riggs found relative shelter, a spot of low ground with enough healthy, sturdy trees to shield them from the brunt of the coming storm. Beau parked near the edge of the copse in case they needed to get out in a hurry. Noisy wind whipped through the branches and whistled through gouges and bullet holes in the body of the truck.

When the rain broke, it came down lightly at first. But within minutes the sullen sky darkened into something fierce and oppressive, taking most of the sickly light with it. The easy patter changed to a heavy thrum, an unsteady sound that changed with the wind. Another few minutes and hail began to fall, beating an even noisier staccato on the roof of the pickup and making Beau grateful they weren't out in the open.

The air was already cooler, and the temperature was likely to drop further still. They just had to wait out the storm's violence. In the meantime, there was nothing they could do, nowhere they could *go*. It wasn't a far leap for Beau's mind to slip into the well-worn tread he'd been worrying at all week.

From the driver's side of the bench, he glanced across the seat and found Riggs staring blankly at the windshield, as if there were anything he could possibly see through that clattering cascade. Riggs had an elbow propped against the door, and his head slouched onto his hand, his entire posture feigning carelessness.

It might even have been convincing if he weren't so carefully *not* looking at Beau.

"How long are we going to do this?" Beau asked, taking his hands off the wheel and glowering.

The question got Riggs's attention hard and fast, and when he turned to meet Beau's stare there was something panic-hot in his eyes. Riggs's hand fell, his arm shifting against the door, and Beau's eyes widened with comprehension. He fumbled behind his own back, locking both doors at once. It wouldn't stop Riggs from simply unlocking his own door and making his escape, but at least the effort would require an extra couple seconds.

Time enough for Beau to blurt, "Seriously? You'd rather chance a concussion and pneumonia than admit you want to fuck me?"

With a barely perceptible flinch, Riggs dropped his hand and gave Beau a resigned look. He still didn't speak.

Beau's glare softened into something more exasperated than angry. "It's okay. Really. You've *got* to know I want the same thing."

Riggs still didn't speak. Instead he turned his eyes forward again, and if anything his expression shuttered further.

Beau swallowed a frustrated sound. "Is it the whole priest thing?" he hazarded, and was surprised when the question earned him a rough fraction of smile.

Riggs still didn't look up, but some of the impossible tightness bled from his posture. "Hell no. I told you, I was a terrible priest. I never met a vow I could keep."

"Is it because we're both men?"

Riggs actually snorted aloud at that, not quite a laugh but close. "No. *God* no. I crossed that bridge years ago. Haven't been too picky between men and women since."

"Then what?" Beau barely resisted the urge to slide closer. "Riggs. *Don*. You've gotta give me something to go on here. If it's not vows, and it's not a sexual identity crisis, then what's your problem?"

For an endless moment, Beau thought Riggs would continue refusing to answer. The hint of smile faded, leaving something stiff and stubborn in its wake. Riggs turned finally, watching Beau with a caution that had no place between them. Motionless but for the drumming of his fingers on his knee.

"Has it occurred to you that I'm more than twice your age?"

Beau blinked. Stared. Waited several seconds for more, only to realize there *wasn't* more. That hadn't been an opening volley; it was the crux of the problem. He didn't know exactly how old Riggs was, but he didn't need to. Beau knew damn well what he wanted. He was just as confident Riggs wanted the same. The gap in their ages made no difference; considering the fucked up state of the world, he couldn't fathom why Riggs should be hung up on it.

"You can't think that actually matters," Beau protested, struggling to understand.

"You're just a kid."

"Fuck you." Beau's mood iced over in an instant. He faced forward to stare at the pounding mess of water on the windshield. Rage blurred his vision, and he reached reflexively for the wheel, fingers curling into angry fists around the hard leather. Suddenly *he* was fighting the urge to open the door and get out of this cab, lightning and hail be damned. He could feel Riggs watching him. He could feel a dozen conflicting emotions ricochet in his own chest, and it took conscious effort to keep his breathing steady. He didn't speak until he could trust himself to find calm enough words, and even then he didn't let go of the wheel. "I'm not a kid. If I were, I'd have been on one of those ships getting off this heap, and I missed that boat *five years ago.*"

Riggs kept silent, but Beau was just getting started.

"Anyway, you don't really think that. If you did, you never would've touched me in the first place. You started this, and you're not that kind of creep." Beau loosened his grip, dropped his hands into his lap. Calm was finding him again, grudgingly. He turned in his seat, and was surprised when Riggs met and held his eyes. Suddenly the cab felt warm, despite the storm and the draft and the pelting hail. "How long have we been watching each other's backs, Don? Just you and me? Two years? Are you really going to try and convince me age means a damn next to that?"

The rigid blank finally eased from Riggs's expression, though the tense set of his spine held. With a spike of comprehension, it occurred to Beau that maybe age wasn't the crux of the problem. A factor, and one clearly giving Riggs pause, but there was a deeper desperation peeking through now. Something both wounded and hopeful, and a little bit terrified. After all, the world had already taken so much from both of them. How could Beau begrudge hesitation in the face of so much loss?

But he wasn't imagining the flash of consideration in those intensely blue eyes, either. Or the softening of stiff posture a moment later, when Riggs asked, "How do I convince you this is a bad idea?"

There was no conviction in the words. Beau allowed himself a small smile as he slid across the bench and—slow enough to allow for protest that did not come—climbed into Riggs's lap.

Spacious as the cab was, this was still a tight fit. The top of Beau's head brushed the ceiling as he settled astride Riggs, his knees digging into the cushion to either side. He braced one hand on the seat back and rested the other lightly over Riggs's heart.

Despite the startled widening of Riggs's eyes, strong fingers curled around Beau's hips to steady him, securing him in place.

"How is this a bad idea?" Beau let his thumb play over bare skin where Riggs's shirt collar gapped open. He couldn't tell if the restless touch was intentional, but he thrilled just the same when Riggs uncurled one hand and pressed it to the small of his back. His pulse sped at the warmth through the thin fabric of his shirt, and he leaned closer without consciously intending to. His gaze kept dropping to Riggs's mouth, despite his best efforts to maintain eye contact.

"Oh, it's not just *one* bad idea." Riggs's voice was already gone to low gravel. "It's half a dozen bad ideas, all wrapped up in one pretty package."

"It's okay if you don't want to fuck me." Beau nuzzled closer, but he didn't kiss Riggs.

Not yet. "We can just... You could let me..." He ghosted his hand lower, teasing past the firm planes of chest and stomach to toy deliberately with the clasp of Riggs's jeans.

It felt like victory when Riggs curled strong fingers around the nape of his neck and dragged him down into a hard kiss. Beau breathed a pleased sound, parting his lips immediately to welcome the intimate thrust of tongue. He still had one hand braced against the seat, but he dropped it now to thread eager fingers through silver hair. Greedy desire lit beneath his skin, making his clothes feel uncomfortably tight, and he pressed nearer, angling for a deeper kiss, pleased when Riggs only held on harder.

Beau stopped teasing at Riggs's fly, sliding the same hand tentatively down to cup him through denim instead. The sound Riggs made—pleased, hungry, muffled against Beau's mouth—was every bit as satisfying as the unmistakable sensation of Riggs stiffening beneath the touch.

Beau curled his hand more surely around rigid heat, and offered just enough pressure to tease.

Then Riggs's hand, the one still resting at the small of Beau's back, lifted away. He didn't have time to protest the loss of contact before Riggs covered his hand between them. Riggs pressed his grip down harder, hips jerking forward so sharply that Beau bumped his head on the ceiling.

Beau broke the kiss with a startled laugh, but Riggs quickly claimed his mouth again, swallowing the laughter right off his tongue.

Then Riggs let go of him in order to tug at *Beau's* zipper, and things went from terrific to even better. They were still kissing, deep and heady, but they were also fumbling in tandem now, a strange sort of race as they struggled with buttons and zips, seeking skin with impatient determination.

Beau succeeded first, slipping his hand past denim and cotton. He was stroking in earnest by the time cool air hit his own cock, alongside the maddening touch of Riggs's hot palm. They broke for air, and Beau curled forward, breathing a fractured gasp of pleasure. The breath in his ear was turning unsteady, and he felt the rise and fall of Riggs's chest as they pressed against each other, never quite close enough. Riggs was cursing softly now, and Beau might have been too, for all he could tell. Too close to the edge to be anything like mindful, he had better things to think about.

Things like the firm, stroking pressure of Riggs's hand; like the sound of Riggs stifling a moan when Beau changed his own rhythm just so; like the mess slicking his fingers as Riggs came for him; like the rush of orgasm cresting beneath Beau's skin, sparking behind his eyelids and carrying him over the edge.

*

Even the most spacious pickup truck was a tight fit for two grown men to get comfortable, especially in the sprawling warmth following their exertions. They managed, sort of, but Riggs was pretty sure he'd landed the raw end of the deal.

Somehow, he wasn't inclined to complain.

He'd slept on the pickup's bench seat before, but he was still surprised by how soft a bed it made, once he managed to find a position without seatbelts digging into his backside. He had to bend his knees against the driver's side door opposite, one leg folded up against the seat back, the other tucked down over the edge. If he fell asleep like this he would be miserable come morning, but he felt fine for the moment.

It might've had something to do with the sated satisfaction lulling his blood. More likely it was Beau's weight stretched out on top of him, long and lazy like a cat. Beau had curled against him once Riggs was settled, the most natural thing in the world. Their bodies fit together like habit, never mind that this was a first between them in almost every way.

Now, with Beau's arm draped sleepily downwards and Beau's breath ghosting warm and steady at his throat, Riggs was half convinced his partner had fallen asleep.

The illusion broke when Beau murmured, "This came out of nowhere for you, didn't it?"

Riggs had one arm looped loosely around Beau's waist, his fingers tracing pointless patterns through the thin T-shirt. With his other hand, he toyed idly with the dark mess of Beau's hair. He fell perfectly still at the question.

"You'll have to be more specific." He wasn't trying to be difficult. He just needed to be sure they were having the same conversation, considering what they'd just gotten up to—and what he hoped they'd get up to again before long.

"I just mean..." Beau's dangling arm lifted, his palm settling high on Riggs's chest. "You never really thought about me before. Not like this."

"Guess I just wasn't paying attention." Riggs tried to keep his voice light. He thought he'd succeeded, but some hint of tension must've snuck through. Above him, Beau pushed up from his chest, peering into his eyes with curious caution.

It was a long moment before Beau asked, "You gonna freak out on me again, or are we good?"

Instead of answering, Riggs tightened his fingers in Beau's hair and tugged him back down, into the kind of slow, teasing kiss they hadn't gotten around to yet. Beau made a pleased sound as his lips parted, and they took their time. Beau had a clever tongue. It made Riggs want to put Beau's mouth to other challenges.

When they finally stopped—when Riggs needed to take a proper breath even more desperately than he needed to keep kissing Beau—neither spoke for several seconds. The cab wasn't silent; there was still too much storm outside. But there was something quiet in the air between them, meaningful and surprisingly intense.

When Riggs finally answered, his voice came out low and rough. "Yeah. We're good."

Beau grinned, then settled against him once more, tucking his head to Riggs's shoulder. Beau's whole body felt easy and loose and perfect, as slow contentment sank into sated limbs.

"What about you?" Riggs asked. "How long have you been thinking about this?"

Beau's pause lasted a beat too long, and when he spoke his answer was deliberately light. "Dunno. A couple weeks, I guess?"

Riggs knew him too well to swallow such an obvious lie, but he didn't press the issue. Instead he kept his tone casual when he retorted, "That long?"

The huff of air Beau breathed could've been a laugh. "I've always had a thing for priests."

*

Beau didn't figure he and Riggs would ever see their unlikely savior trio again. A scavenging lifestyle didn't exactly encourage long-term acquaintances. The only familiar faces they ever encountered were those at the trading sites and settlements where they returned frequently to barter. Even those faces tended to change and disappear without warning, but that too was to be expected. A farmer's life was challenging enough without a poisoned sky and deadened soil to contend with. Beau had thought about it plenty, and he still had trouble imagining the patience it must take to coax food out of the ground under such conditions.

It didn't stop him idly yearning to stay put for a while, but it did prevent him from trying too hard to argue Riggs around.

Plain stupid chance brought their path once more across the three people who had saved their asses so spectacularly. It happened three months after their memorable first meeting, and there was no gunfire this time. No falling trees. Just familiar faces on a rutted patch of dirt, mutual surprise in a wash of purple dusk. Snow dusted the ground, but that didn't stop the reunited parties from lighting and sharing a campfire in a relatively dry ditch. Beau didn't have to search far in his memory for the three names. Yuko, Mel, Sammy. They were burned pretty brightly into his mind. Dramatic rescue apparently had that effect.

"Where're you boys headed?" Yuko asked them. The shadows were heavy on her face as she reached around the fire to pass dishes of stew to Mel and then Sammy in turn.

"Marwood." Riggs accepted the plate she handed him next. "Truck's acting up. Last time we went through they had some parts for trade."

Marwood was two days out at their current pace, and Beau would just as soon they were there already. Whatever was troubling the engine, it wasn't something their supply of spare parts could remedy. He needed a second set of eyes and a wider armament of tools, and the thought of getting stranded two days out from those things wasn't a heartening one.

"We're going the same way," Mel said between mouthfuls of her dinner. "Maybe we could stick together the next couple days? If you want."

Beau definitely wanted that. There was a lot to be said for the insurance policy of extra people who you could be confident wouldn't stab you in your sleep. The gaggle of three drove an SUV that seemed rougher around the edges than Riggs and Beau's truck, but it looked sturdy enough. Maybe if the truck didn't make it, the three would be willing to carry a message and some goods the rest of the distance, in exchange for a fair cut.

Practical as all these considerations were, Beau focused on his own dinner and didn't get his hopes up. Riggs was too much a loner to agree.

"Sure," Riggs said.

Beau's head snapped up in surprise, his eyes wide as they locked on the quiet amusement of Riggs's expression.

It wasn't until hours later, when the three heroes were all tucked into their own vehicle, and Beau had put up the thermal tent for himself and Riggs, that he had the chance for questions. He waited until they were both settled and warm, until Riggs was a reassuring line of heat curled close along his back and Riggs's arm was tucked snugly around him beneath the blankets.

Then, finally, Beau asked the question that had been burning at him all night. "Since when do you trust people who aren't me?"

Riggs was silent a long time before answering. "I don't trust them, exactly." He sounded like he was working it through even as he spoke. "But they did us a solid once, when they had no reason to stick their necks out. I figure they're honest, and it *is* safer to travel in a group."

"Huh." Beau didn't argue the point. The last thing he wanted was to talk Riggs out of a perfectly reasonable decision.

*

By some string of fortune, the truck made it without incident the entire way to Marwood. Two days' travel with near strangers didn't grate at Riggs nearly as badly as he might've expected, and fortune was still with them when they opened their truck bed to trade. Beau was able to track down the parts and tools he needed to beat the sullen engine block into submission, and they got good value for the scrap that remained.

There were no drawn-out goodbyes as their three casual companions went about their own business, though Mel pulled Riggs aside before leaving town to let him know they'd be passing through Camp Stanton, Cold Stop, and Norfolk in the next couple months. Riggs was surprised to realize he wanted to return the favor, but he and Beau rarely had a solid plan. It was mostly gut instinct that steered their path. But he thanked her for the information and promised to keep his ears open. She smiled, clearly not offended by the lack of reciprocity, and shook his hand.

He and Beau were hours later in leaving, thanks to the extra repairs, but they still departed well ahead of sunset. It was barely snowing, but even in the cab of the pickup they were both wearing coats and gloves.

"Think we'll see them again?" Beau asked, eyes on the path ahead though Riggs was driving. Beau had his legs kicked up on the dashboard in a comfortable sprawl, and Riggs only spared him a glance before focusing once more on the ground ahead.

"Probably."

It wasn't just chance or instinct that brought their paths together at Cold Stop, and from the look on Mel's face—pleased and smug all at once—she knew it damn well. Yuko actually hugged them this time, squashing affection that Beau accepted easily and Riggs tolerated with stiff patience. Even Sammy seemed glad to see them, in his quiet, spindly way.

They stayed more deliberately in touch after that. Riggs rarely protested when Beau insisted they speed their pace to meet the three at another unofficial rendezvous. It *was* nice, Riggs conceded in the privacy of his own head, having familiar faces to look forward to. Beau was more than enough company on the road, and hell, Riggs preferred solitude most of the time. He liked having license to touch Beau however and whenever they liked. But it was also pleasant to have someone else to talk to once in a while. Someone with different sources of news, different recipes for the dull food that comprised every meal, different ideas about where to go next.

They began to travel together off-and-on, for more than just a fleeting day or two in passing. Some regions were safer as a team effort, and Riggs had to reevaluate before long; he *did* trust their new friends. It was a startling revelation.

The rest of winter passed that way, sporadic companions on the long road. It made the coldest months of scarcity easier to fend through. Sharing their own stock from time to time might have seemed a hardship, but the trio was happy to return the favor when February saw Riggs and Beau short on supplies. They had learned each other's preferred paths and trading routes, habits, and hideaways. Never mind that Riggs and Beau still never followed anything so solid as a plan; somehow Yuko and Mel would track them down anyway, Sammy always in tow.

When spring arrived and moved into summer, there didn't seem much reason to change what had proven a reliable strategy. And for once, when autumn settled in hard and cool, Riggs didn't find himself fretting over winter's worst case scenarios.

They met in November, at a bend in the Platte River, both en route to Hope. Riggs had always thought it an idiotic name for a town, and his opinion remained unchanged.

"I hear they got an honest-to-fuck apple tree to grow," Sammy said when they all stopped to eat—nothing but canned food scavenged from a warehouse cellar a couple weeks back—and to refuel both vehicles from their respective stores.

"Bullshit," Beau muttered around a mouthful of limp vegetables. Riggs was inclined to agree with him.

Sammy shrugged his skinny shoulders and exchanged a look with Mel. There was no point arguing about it. They'd reach

Hope soon enough, and see for themselves if the unlikely rumors were true.

They made good time that afternoon. Good enough that the sun was still high when they got close enough to see steady plumes of smoke blowing slant-ward across the sky. Riggs, behind the wheel, nudged Beau with an elbow.

"I see it." Beau leaned forward as if for a better look.

Riggs braked and rolled his window down, waited for the SUV to pull up alongside and do the same.

"That's a lot of smoke," Yuko said in a tight, worried tone.

Riggs nodded. Too much smoke. That was no bonfire. They should turn around. Pick a different direction to drive—one less likely to lead them into a fight—find a new place to trade their latest collection of scavenge. Beau wouldn't be happy about it. The others probably wouldn't either, considering the stubbornly heroic way they'd first introduced themselves. But avoiding unnecessary danger was the only practical choice.

Which meant Riggs had no explanation for the fact that his next words were, "Let's pick up the pace. Everyone, stay on guard."

Yuko gave him a look that said she didn't appreciate him giving orders and stating the obvious, but she nodded just the same. Through the open window he saw her check the cartridges in her shotgun, then turn and mumble something to Mel. To Riggs's right, Beau rolled down his own window and reached for the rifle beneath the seat. Riggs started driving as soon as Beau had the weapon in hand.

"This is going to be bad." Beau's eyes scanned restlessly ahead, checked the mirrors, watched the horizon.

"Don't borrow trouble," Riggs retorted, but his heart wasn't in it. This *would* be bad.

Problem was, he had no idea what kind of threat they were driving into.

*

Riggs caught sight of open flames well before he and Beau reached the high-fenced edge of the town. By the time both vehicles stopped, as close as they dared drive, the sky was smothered with pluming smoke. Riggs bit back a curse and grabbed a clean rag from the duffel beneath the driver's seat. He tied it around his head, covering his nose and mouth like a bandit. The mask would be barely any protection, but it was the best he could do. He tossed a second rag to Beau who did the same, then descended from the truck.

They separated from the other three, Beau and Riggs circling west, while Yuko and Mel led Sammy the opposite direction until they were out of sight. Riggs had his revolver loaded and steady in his hands, and every step he took was wary. In his peripheral vision, Beau held the rifle against his shoulder with all the confident caution of a man prepared for the worst.

The first bodies were only a few paces from open ground. They'd been shot in the back, Riggs noted when he got close enough to check for nonexistent pulses. They'd been running for their lives and hadn't made it. Blood soaked the dirt and brown grass, the stench of death mixing viciously with stinging smoke. Riggs signaled to Beau to keep moving, and they continued forward, avoiding the worst of the flames, both ready to break for cover at the first hint of danger.

They found no danger, but plenty of death.

There were more bodies as they moved past fields and farms into a more crowded cluster of buildings. The dead were bloodied and bludgeoned and riddled with bullets.

There must have been some two hundred people living here, Riggs guessed, and the thought raised bile at the back of his throat. He wondered if anyone had gotten out, but his gut—and the bodies he and Beau had passed—suggested not.

He checked for a pulse at every throat, always without success. They couldn't afford to stay here long. The fire was spreading—gradually, yes, but spreading just the same—and Riggs had no intention of being present when it closed in.

"What do you think happened?" Beau asked as Riggs got to his feet.

"Thieves," Riggs answered grimly. Anger kept his voice quiet. The tears in his eyes were all from the thickening smoke, but that didn't mean he felt any less for the dead. No one should have to die this way.

As they retreated along a different path than the route they'd followed in, a gurgling whisper stopped them short.

Beau was the one who caught the quiet sounds, and he hesitated, grabbed Riggs by the sleeve of his coat. "Did you hear that?"

Riggs turned, braced for an attack. What he found instead was a man on his stomach, shuddering and bleeding into the dirt, not even looking at them. Riggs put his gun away, trusting Beau to have his back, and hurried to the man's side. He dropped to his knees and set a hand to one trembling shoulder.

The man froze, then shuddered harder, twisting painfully to peer up at him.

"Who're you people?" the man demanded in a rattling voice. Riggs didn't bother asking Beau to look him over; there was too much death in those widening eyes.

"We came to trade." Riggs withdrew his hand and wished there were something he could do to make the man more comfortable. "What happened here?"

The man shook but somehow managed to push himself further upright. He was clutching his stomach with one hand. That seemed to be where most of the blood was coming from. Riggs didn't look too closely. He kept his eyes on the man's face, on his struggle to breathe the smoke-laden air.

"They came for our winter reserves." The man choked, spitting blood into the dirt. "Must've figured when we'd be done stockpiling. I never seen so many cutthroats work together like that."

"How many?" Riggs demanded.

"Dozens. More maybe, I don't know. By the time the alarm came through, they had us completely surrounded. Didn't matter how many more of us there were, they just killed and killed and killed."

"Did anyone make it out?"

"No." That one word carried spirit-broken pain, and Riggs set his hand on the man's shoulder again.

"Do you know where they went?"

The man's dying eyes sharpened, and to his left Riggs could feel Beau looking at him the same way. It was an idiotic question. What point was there in knowing where a band that size had traveled to, other than to avoid them? Five people certainly couldn't do a damn thing but annoy them, and get themselves killed in the process.

But the man answered anyway, eventually and with a renewed edge of agony. "There's another town. Not much bigger than ours, northeast along the river."

"Farrow," Riggs murmured, and the man gave a pained nod.

"I couldn't hear much of what they said, but that's a name I caught more than once." The man let go of his ruined stomach then, and grabbed at the front of Riggs's jacket. Blood and thicker fluids smeared into the fabric, but Riggs didn't protest. The man's face was almost purple with exertion, and the words carried the last of his strength. "I got a sister settled up that way. Those thieves can't have got far, not this fast. Not traveling with so many on foot. You might get there first if you cut straight west and go the long way 'round Mason's Rock."

Riggs knew the landmark, a bald jut of stone that stood twice as tall as a man, alone in a wide stretch of nothing. He and Beau had passed it more than once in the past, on their own way to Farrow.

Before Riggs could do or say anything stupid, the man's hand fell away and he doubled over in fresh agony. Riggs hovered close, hating that there was nothing he could do.

"Do you want last rites?" he asked, the only paltry offering he had.

But the man only laughed—a wet, gruesome wheeze—and shook his head. "No, thanks. I never was a big believer in Heaven."

Another minute, maybe less, and the man fell still. Riggs checked his pulse, already knowing he would find nothing there. He shook his head as he stood. His chest felt tight and wrong.

"*Fuck*," Beau breathed behind him, and the word was heavy with anger.

"Come on." Riggs turned his steps in the direction that should take them straight back to their truck. "We've got to move fast."

Beau fell into hurried step beside him, but Riggs knew it wasn't their pace that made him sound winded when he asked, "We're going to warn Farrow?"

"We're damn well going to *try*," Riggs snapped, and ran faster still.

*

It would have been a slaughter.

Without the warning, Farrow would unquestionably have fallen just like Hope. As it was, Beau didn't like their chances, especially when Riggs insisted on staying to fight. Somehow it didn't surprise him when Mel announced that she, Yuko, and Sammy would stick around, too.

Five steady gun hands were a strong advantage, but doubt gnawed at Beau's insides just the same. It couldn't possibly be enough. Even with Farrow's watch posts and sentries, its citizenry armed and ready, they were facing off against an enemy that had already razed one community to the ground. What hope was there against an army—even a small one—with better weapons, a penchant for fire, and no interest in leaving survivors?

When the band of thieves crested the rise—in numbers even more staggering than the dying man from Hope had guessed—Farrow was armed and ready to meet them.

Beau jumped when Riggs snuck up behind him in the last moments of looming quiet. Riggs's warmth pressed along his spine, hand slipping forward to rest over Beau's stomach, not quite an embrace.

Riggs's words tickled the shell of Beau's ear. "Just so you know? If you get yourself killed today, you and I'll be fighting 'til the sun burns out." Beau didn't ask how that was even possible. He just turned far enough around to twist his fingers in Riggs's hair and steal a brief kiss. It was all the reassurance they had time for. That was when the enemy attacked.

The fighting lasted two full days, straight through the night and out the other side. There were fleeting moments of stillness broken by shouts and screams and the rapid-fire staccato of bullets. It was the war all over again, and Beau had to put his gun down and take up a roll of bandages well before the battle ceased. It burned, having to hang back from the fighting, not knowing where Riggs was, or if he was even alive. But it was exactly like Riggs had once said: some things you don't get to turn your back on.

It was nearly nightfall the second evening when the last of the gunfire stopped and the final flames were smothered. Beau hadn't slept in over forty-eight hours, but he didn't stop. He kept working until there were no more wounded waiting for him, and even then he couldn't shake the feeling that there should be more he could do.

"Hey." Riggs's voice, and that one syllable shot straight through Beau, loosening the fearful tension that had been choking him.

"Hey, hey, easy. Put the gauze down and let's get some rest."

"You're not hurt?" Beau rounded on him, eyes raking the length of Riggs's body in search of harm. Riggs wasn't wearing his coat. There was a clean bandage cinched tight around one bare forearm, and a lazy trickle of blood drying at his right temple. "Here, let me." Beau crouched again, found a fresh cloth and what remained of his bottle of clean water. Riggs gave him an exasperated look, but he let Beau wash the blood away and examine the shallow gash, which was already scabbing over and clearly not life-threatening.

"Come *on*," Riggs muttered when Beau finally set the first aid supplies aside. He waited just long enough for Beau to discard the thin gloves he'd been wearing, then grabbed him by the elbow and aimed him toward the center of town.

Everything seemed built of shadows in the settling dusk. A couple of larger buildings had been hastily converted to accommodate a whole lot of tired, injured people, and it was into one of these that Riggs steered him. There were cots and benches and rumpled bedrolls in every possible corner of a huge room. The air was surprisingly warm. For all that the walls looked to be patch-worked together from uneven concrete and scrap metal, there was little draft from outside. A round hearth stood at the center of the enormous room, surrounded by several long benches, most of them occupied. Beau wondered if this was the town hall. Smoke rose from a steady fire in that hearth, up through a gap in the high ceiling.

"Cozy." Beau tried to sound wry, but he was too bleary.

"This way." Riggs must have looked into the whole *sleep* question before he came for

Beau, because he directed now like a man with purpose, straight for one of the only open bedrolls in the entire room. It wasn't quite wide enough for two people, but that had never stopped them before. Beau settled in with an exhausted sigh, scooting to the edge so that Riggs could curl in close behind him with a blanket.

"You did good." Riggs pressed the words into Beau's throat like a kiss. He draped an arm forward, wrapping it snugly around Beau's waist beneath the blanket that covered them both.

"Thanks." The word came out fuzzy and smudged, but Beau forced himself to stay conscious long enough to ask, "The others?"

"Yuko and Mel are fine, and Sammy will be soon enough. Stop thinking so hard and *sleep*." The admonishment was gentle, but Beau didn't need it. He was already fading.

*

Beau woke chilly, alone, and reluctant to open his eyes. His head throbbed, and when he tried to swallow, his throat protested the effort, parched and raw. His whole body ached like he'd been drinking heavily the night before.

He sat upright carefully, wary of the way even slight motion sharpened the pounding at his temples. He kept his eyes closed until the discomfort eased, and then opened them with unsteady caution.

His canteen was on the floor beside him, and he blinked at it in surprise. It was heavy when he took it in hand. Beau couldn't remember if he'd been carrying it when Riggs found him, but he was damn sure it shouldn't be full. Riggs had been up for ages without waking him, then. Beau scowled at the thought, but didn't hesitate to unscrew the lid of the canteen. The water inside was lukewarm, but it was clean and fresh, and Beau drank greedily.

It was with reluctance that he twisted the cap back on and set the canteen aside, belatedly taking in his surroundings. The room looked much the same as it had the night before. Despite the autumn chill, the front doors had been thrown wide to let cloudy daylight through. Fire still burned in the enormous circle of the central hearth.

His searching eyes found Riggs quickly, standing near the door in conversation with a restless woman. Beau rose and crossed the space with careful steps, mindful of other bodies sprawled in sleep. He couldn't figure out why the woman was moving the way she was—swaying, almost bouncing with every breath—like she couldn't figure out how to hold still.

Neither Riggs nor the woman seemed to notice his approach, and Beau caught the murmured words of private conversation.

"—good of you, Mister Riggs. I wish my Andrew could've met you. Oh, hello. You must be Beau." Her eyes found Beau with that last, a warm smile of greeting crossing her face. Her gaze darted between the two men as Beau took a final step to stand beside Riggs.

"Morning, ma'am," he said, feeling awkward for intruding.

"Trudy," she supplied kindly. "And this is Mayra." For the first time Beau noticed the bundle she was holding in her arms, and abruptly he understood her constant motion.

"That's... a baby." He gawped, startled and awed and just a little bit disbelieving. But that was definitely a baby in the woman's arms, its eyes wide open and staring about with an infant's bright intensity. Trudy smiled with obvious amusement, and when Beau turned to Riggs he was surprised to find a similar expression on his partner's face. Embarrassed at his own rudeness, Beau fought down a blush and said, "She's beautiful."

"Thank you." Trudy's eyes fell to the infant, and suddenly there was sadness in her smile. "I wish I could have her baptized. Andrew wanted that more than anything. I promised, when he died, but I can't remember the last time a preacher came through these parts."

Beau glanced too quickly at Riggs, then felt immediately guilty that he might have given away a secret that wasn't his to share.

Riggs didn't look angry, though. If anything, the quiet smile on his face widened. "I'd be honored to do it." A pause, a glint in his eye, and he added, "That is, if you'll accept the help of a priest who gave up the cloth a long time ago."

Trudy stared at him for a long, *long* time. Long enough to make Beau wonder if she might refuse.

When she nodded, there were tears softening the corners of her eyes. "That'd be kind of you, Father. I'll hold you to it before you go."

She departed not much later, with a backward glance over her shoulder.

"Who is she?" Beau watched her disappear into the crowd-clogged center of the town.

"She's the mayor, more or less. She came to thank us for bringing the warning."

"Huh." She was out of sight now, but Beau still watched the milling movement of exhausted townsfolk outside. Without looking directly at Riggs, he said, "You did good, too. I don't think I've ever seen anyone so grateful." He didn't mean the warning, or the fighting, or any of the past two days. He meant a moment ago, in the cloud-dulled morning light, when Riggs offered his service for no other reason than kindness. From the way Beau's words made his partner fall silent, Riggs followed his meaning.

Several wordless minutes passed before Riggs said, in a softer voice, "She also said the town council welcomes us, for as long as we'd like to stay."

"You don't want to stay." Beau knew as much already. Riggs never wanted to stay. He was probably itching even now to get back to their truck, back on the road with fresh supplies.

"I might not completely hate the idea."

Beau turned so suddenly his neck twinged, peering at Riggs in open shock. He found Riggs watching him with a warm expression, mouth quirked up at one side, eyes alive with something like mischief. He wasn't teasing, though. Those words had been completely earnest, and there was something somber beneath the signs of subdued mirth.

"You *never* want to stay," Beau protested in helpless confusion.

"I'm just saying, it might be worth thinking about after all." Riggs gave a shrug that was anything but careless. "Maybe we stick around, help them rebuild a little. We can ditch when we get restless, or when the weather warms up. Whichever comes first."

Beau tried not to stare, but he failed. The thought of staying put for even a matter of weeks, never mind the whole of winter like Riggs was hinting... Beau honestly couldn't wrap his head around the possibility.

He liked the idea a whole lot.

"You're serious?" he checked, even though Riggs would never have said it otherwise. "You really want to do this?"

Riggs's smile softened, and he took a step into Beau's space. "If you want to, I'm willing to try."

THE END

ABOUT THE AUTHOR

Yolande Kleinn may be a shameless dreamer and a stubborn optimist, but she is also a proud purveyor of erotic romance. Excitable, fastidious and a little eclectic, she spends every spare moment writing the stories she wants to read. If she can drag other people into the pool along with her, then so much the better.

You can find Yolande via her website:
yolandekleinn.com

OTHER TITLES BY YOLANDE

A BRAND NEW
PATCH OF SKY

Starship pilot Mitch Kato doesn't make a habit of pining for the impossible. He's always kept tight hold on the inconvenient feelings he harbors for his captain, Solomon Finn. But when a close scrape grounds Sol's ship and threatens to scatter the crew, Mitch finds himself making an unexpected promise. As he and Sol consider a different trajectory, Mitch wonders if their longstanding friendship might be the beginning of something more.

EVERY SECOND YOU'RE ALIVE

Major Franklin Cade has spent years fighting the undead scourge that drove humanity from Earth. Now victory is in sight, but it's come at immeasurable cost. He has sacrificed everything in the line of duty—even his own heart.

For six months Lieutenant Daniel Mendoza has been missing in action. Only stubbornness and a refusal to tarnish Mendoza's memory have kept Franklin alive since losing the man he wouldn't admit he loved.

When a perilous rescue needs volunteers, he returns to the canyon where Mendoza fell. He is not prepared for the hope that ignites as he follows a fading distress signal across infested terrain. In the shadow of a deadly countdown every second is precious, but Franklin refuses to lose Mendoza again.

AN INTIMATE CHARADE

Cargo ship captain Galin Odona is in desperate need of a contract. When a lucrative opportunity comes his way, he invites Addison Valdez—smart, stubborn, and the only Human member of his crew—to join the negotiation.

Anatoria Baell's contract is not precisely legal, and she has unconventional methods for choosing where to put her trust. Galin agrees to pose as a distant relation during a gathering at her private estate. The negotiation takes a complicated turn when Addison proclaims that Galin is not only his captain, but his mate. The hot-headed lie puts them in a tough spot, maintaining their charade for the duration.

But Galin is a terrible liar. Even worse, he's been in love with Addison for years. Now, through tight quarters and an illusion of intimacy, he must win the contract without giving himself away. The task seems monumental, but Galin cannot afford to fail.

SOMETHING BORROWED

When public defender Trevor Ortega finds himself dateless for his ex's wedding, faking a relationship seems like the perfect solution. Less perfect is his thoughtless impulse to invite Sebastian Greer—friend, federal judge, and former boss—as his plus one. It would be a solid plan if not for one problem: Trevor's been in love with Sebastian for years, and each fraudulent touch will remind him of everything he can't have.

Trevor doesn't know why Sebastian agreed to his scheme, but there's no backing out now. It's only one night after all, and what's a little heartbreak between friends?

OPEN SKIES

After seven years working as partners, Kai and Ilsa are the best professional finders in the business. There's nothing they can't track down, no matter how unfamiliar the star system or hazardous the path. When a new client insists on accompanying the search for his daughter, Ilsa and Kai reluctantly agree. How can they refuse when Eleazar Dantes is desperate enough to pay double their usual fee?

But a high-stakes investigation is no time for distractions. Even more troublesome, when Kai realizes his true feelings for Ilsa, his timing couldn't be worse. Never mind that she doesn't seem to reciprocate: heartbreak is the least of their problems as the trail they're following grows dangerous.

With every step forward, Kai and Ilsa are more certain they won't find Eleazar's missing daughter alive.

COVET

Jack Mason—graphic designer and unrepentant player—has never been interested in monogamy. He certainly isn't looking for romance when he meets Professor Colin Sloan.

Newly single and not looking for anything serious, Colin is intrigued by Jack's offer of a physical affair with no strings attached. Becoming friends wasn't part of the plan, but as accidents go, this one's pretty great.

Peter Mason is Jack's identical twin. In a long-term relationship himself, Peter tells no one that he's falling for his brother's newest favorite, even as the secret creates tension with his girlfriend.

When Peter's relationship falls apart, he seduces Colin, fully expecting Jack to forgive his transgression. But Jack is keeping secrets too—he hasn't told even Colin that he's fallen in love. Suddenly the twins are feuding, and Colin is caught in the middle, blindsided by the revelation that he doesn't want to choose between them.

Now all three must find a way to share, or they'll tear each other apart.

WONDERLY WROTH

Arthur knows he is destined to die at Camlann. But when the Lady Merlin enlists a powerful enchantment to save him—an enchantment to tether Arthur's life to Lancelot's—the magic carries unintended consequences. Lancelot's strength could be Arthur's salvation, but what of the deeper connection that now binds the king to his most loyal knight? The connection is only temporary, but when Arthur learns the truth of Lancelot's feelings for him, their friendship could change forever.

RIGHT HERE WITH ME

Jessa Nolli doesn't like to admit how much of a giver she is beneath the wry exterior. Heck, she gave her heart to her best friend years ago and still hasn't fessed up. How can she, when Amaia has no earthly reason to love her back?

Amaia Campos has landed a full ride scholarship to her dream school. There's only one problem: college means moving clear across the country, two thousand miles from her family and friends. The worst part is leaving Jessa behind without ever admitting how she feels.

A road trip is either exactly what they need or a disaster in the making. Faced with three days on the road—with nonstop driving, a box full of cacti, and only one bed—Jessa and Amaia have one last chance to get this right before everything changes forever.

SIMPLE AFTER ALL

Noah Fiore, contracts attorney and dedicated curmudgeon, spends every Christmas with his family on the shore of Lake Superior. It's practically tradition for his sister to invite some lonely acquaintance along for the festivities.

But this year's guest is no pity case. Riley Coto is a friend, whose warmth and charm instantly win over the collective hearts of the Fiore family—all except Noah, who remains as dour and unapproachable as ever.

Riley finds himself inexplicably drawn to Noah. Something tells him there's more to the man than stubborn work ethic and bad attitude. With Christmas fast approaching, Riley is falling for Noah, and there's nothing simple about that.

www.ingramcontent.com/pod-product-compliance
Lightning Source LLC
Chambersburg PA
CBHW051950170626
46808CB00007B/2555